CLACKYMUCKY
AND THE BULLDOG

小鴨奇奇
和鬥牛犬

Josephine Croser 著

Carol McLean-Carr 繪

本局編輯部 譯

ᗰ 三民書局

Ted was an old, old **bulldog**.
Each day he **snoozed** on the grass near a tree
in the far, far corner of the garden.
His nose tickled with the smells of spring.
His ears twitched with the **hum** of bees.
And his brown eyes opened, this way and that,
as he watched the ducks on the pond.

Near Ted's tree, where **nasturtiums** grew,
Daphne laid one egg each day.
When the nest was full, she sat on the eggs
and dreamed of the ducklings to come.
Webster settled beside his **mate**
and dreamed of the worms in the pond!

bulldog
[ˋbʊlˌdɔg]
名 鬥牛犬

snooze
[snuz]
動 打盹

hum
[hʌm]
名 嗡嗡聲

nasturtium
[næ`stɝʃəm]
名 金蓮花

mate
[met]
名 配偶

泰德是一隻老態龍鍾的鬥牛犬。他每天都躲到花園裡的偏僻角落，在樹旁的草地上打盹兒。春天的氣息搔得他的鼻子好癢，蜜蜂嗡嗡的聲音害得他的耳朵不停抽動。泰德睜著他那雙棕色的眼睛，眼珠子跟著池塘裡的鴨群轉啊轉的。

在泰德的那棵樹旁，金蓮花盛開，妮妮每天在這兒下一顆蛋。等巢裡裝滿了蛋，她便坐到這些蛋上頭，夢想著鴨寶寶的誕生。而妮妮的老公韋伯，則在一旁想著池塘裡的蟲蟲。

The weeks went by and the days grew warm
until one **stormy** night it rained.
Ted lay inside, **snug** and warm by the fire.
Outside on the nest the ducks **huddled** down.
"Pip-pip," they could hear from the eggs!
When morning came Ted paused at the door.
The air smelled **crisp** and clean.
Then, **dragging** his old **mat** down to the tree,
he saw that some ducklings had **hatched**.

stormy
[`stɔrmɪ]
形 狂風暴雨的

snug
[snʌg]
形 舒服的

huddle
[`hʌdl̩]
動 縮成一團

幾個星期過去了，天氣逐漸暖和，直到有天晚上刮起了狂風暴雨。泰德躺在屋裡的爐火旁，烤得暖洋洋的。屋外的鴨子在巢裡縮成一團。那些蛋傳出「啵！啵！」的聲音哩！天亮了，泰德在門口停下腳步，空氣聞起來乾淨又清爽。然後泰德拖著那條陪伴他多年的老蓆子來到樹下，他發現有幾隻小鴨已經孵出來了。

They were **fluffy** and gold.
Webster, the **drake, nudged** them back with his **bill**
as they started to run and **explore**.
Suddenly he nudged too hard,
bumping Daphne as she **stretched**.
Her foot knocked the very last egg
and it rolled and **spun** out of sight.
Daphne **wobbled** her tail and quacked.
Then she led the way down to the pond.

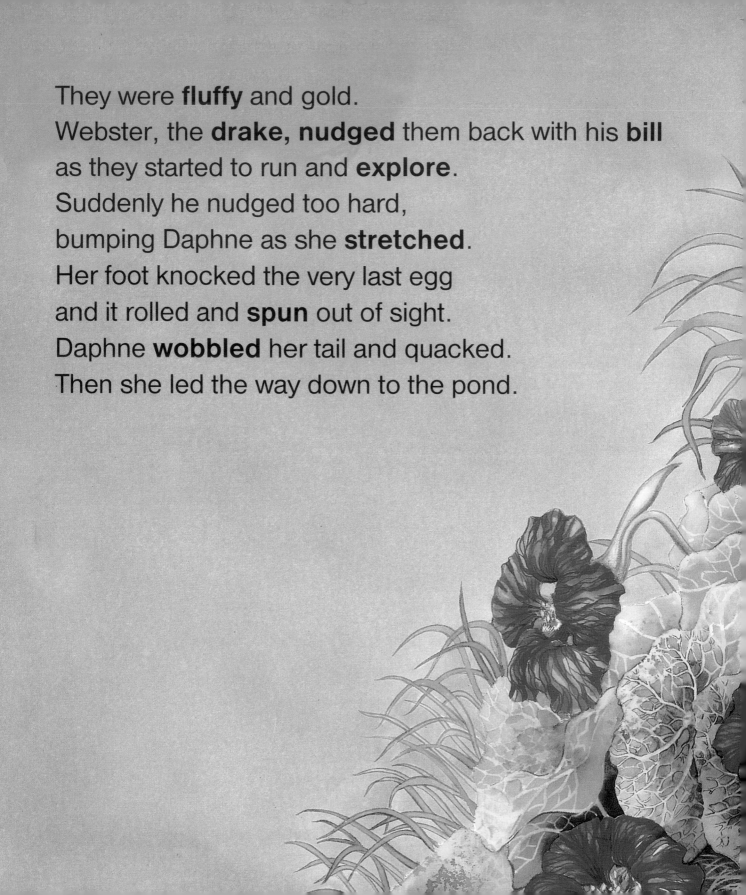

fluffy
[`flʌfɪ]
形 毛茸茸的

drake
[drek]
名 公鴨

nudge
[nʌdʒ]
動 輕推

bill
[bɪl]
名 鳥喙

explore
[ɪk`splor]
動 探索

stretch
[strɛtʃ]
動 伸懶腰

他們是一群金黃色毛茸茸的小東西。小鴨子們蹦蹦跳跳地想到處探索，他們的老爹韋伯便用他的嘴輕輕地將他們推回去。突然，他用力過猛，撞上了正在伸懶腰的妮妮，妮妮的腳碰到了最後一顆還沒孵出的蛋，結果這顆蛋一下子便咕嚕咕嚕滾得不見了蹤影。妮妮搖著尾巴呱呱叫，然後帶頭往池塘走去。

spin
[spɪn]
動 旋轉

wobble
[`wabḷ]
動 搖晃

12
13

The last egg **bumped** on a stone as it rolled
and out of the **shell crawled** Clackymucky!

The bees buzzed. Ted **yawned**,
and his eyes *seemed* shut.
Then **silence** filled the corner.
Clackymucky looked at a **toadstool**.
She looked at a spider in its web.
She **blinked** her ink-black eyes
and felt small, and very alone.

A **shadow** moved along the **fence**.

shell
[ʃɛl]
名 蛋殼

bump
[bʌmp]
動 撞到

crawl
[krɔl]
動 爬

最後那顆蛋滾啊滾的撞上了石頭，接著，奇奇便從蛋殼裡爬了出來。

蜜蜂嗡嗡嗡地飛來飛去，泰德打了個呵欠，眼睛好像閉了起來，這兒一片靜悄悄地。奇奇盯著一棵草菇看了一會兒，又瞧了瞧網中的蜘蛛，她眨著烏黑的雙眼，覺得自己好渺小，好孤獨哦！

這時，一道黑影沿著籬笆移動過來。

Suddenly there was **movement** everywhere.

The cat **pounced**.

The dog **rushed**.

The duckling fell on her face!

Then over the fence went the cat in a **scamper**,
back to the yard of the house next door.

Ted's **growl rumbled** in his throat and
Clackymucky **peered** through the grass.

Now she was not alone!

She had found a friend.

Ted turned and **swaggered** back to his tree.

Clackymucky followed him!

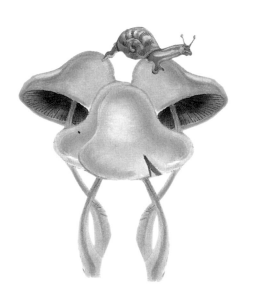

movement
[`muvmənt]
名 動作

pounce
[pauns]
動 飛撲

rush
[rʌʃ]
動 猛衝

scamper

[`skæmpɚ]

名 逃走

growl

[graul]

名 吼叫聲

rumble

[`rʌmbl̩]

動 隆隆作響

忽然間，到處都動了起來。貓兒撲上前來，狗兒猛衝過來，小鴨子臉朝地上跌了一跤！然後，貓兒越過籬笆，退回隔壁的院子。泰德隆隆地低吼著，奇奇躲在草叢中盯著他看。現在她不孤單了！她找到了一個朋友。泰德轉身昂首闊步回到那棵樹下，奇奇一步一步跟了過去。

peer

[pɪr]

動 盯著看

swagger

[`swægɚ]

動 昂首闊步

Later, when Ted went inside,
Clackymucky skipped and **tripped** behind him.
And when Ted **spilled** some **gravy** from his bowl,
Clackymucky **paddled** in it and left **footprints**
over the floor.

trip
[trɪp]
動 輕快地走

spill
[spɪl]
動 灑出

一會兒，泰德走進屋裡，奇奇蹦蹦跳跳地跟在後頭。接著，泰德把肉汁從碗裡潑灑出來；奇奇踩著地上的湯汁玩，弄得地板上到處都是她的腳印子。

gravy
[`grevɪ]
名 肉汁

paddle [`pædl̩]
動 在淺水啪噠啪噠地走

footprint
[`fut͵prɪnt]
名 腳印

All was calm that night as Ted **snored** on his **rug**.
For a while he slept well.
Then a tiny sound began which grew louder
and louder until it seemed to fill the room.

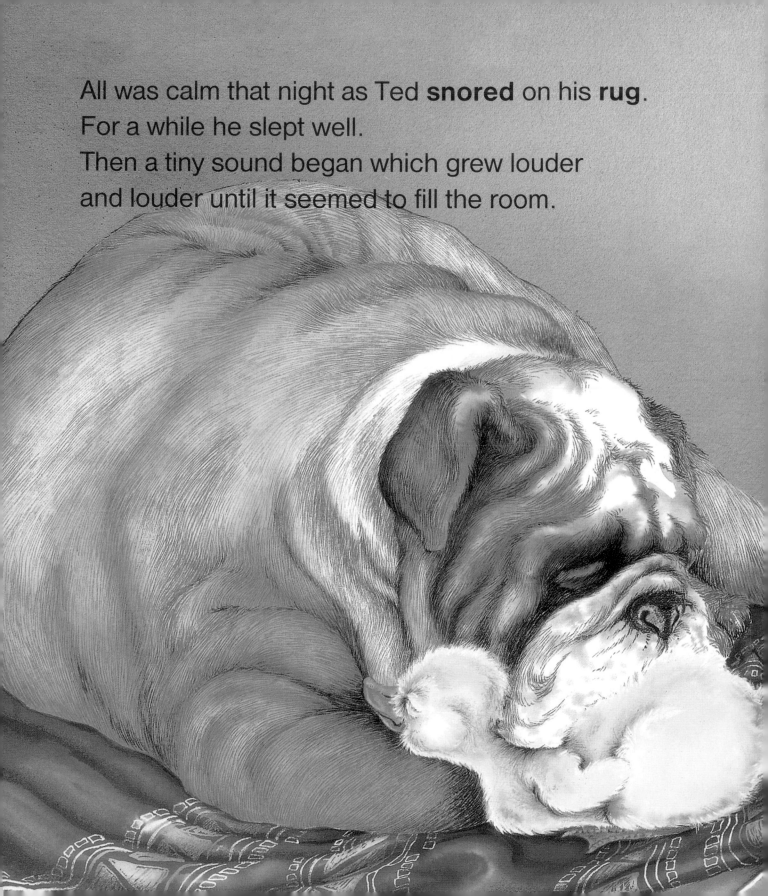

"Pip… Pip… Pip.. Pip.
PIP. PIP. PIP. PIP. PIP!"
Ted pushed his nose into the duckling's box
and touched a little cold bill.
He **nuzzled** the water bag that had grown cool,
and felt the tiny duckling pushing against his **cheek**.
Gently he **tipped** the box with his **paw**
and Clackymucky crawled out and
slept beneath his chin.

snore

[snor]

動 打鼾

rug

[rʌg]

名 毯子

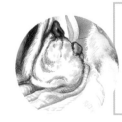

nuzzle

[`nʌzl̩]

動 用鼻子摩擦

cheek
[tʃik]
名 臉頰

gently
[ˋdʒɛntlɪ]
副 輕輕地

那天晚上，泰德趴在他的毯子上打鼾，一切都很平靜。泰德睡得真香甜，可是不一會兒，一個微弱的聲音傳過來，聲音越來越大，到最後整個房間都是這個聲音。

「啵—啵—啵—啵⋯⋯！」泰德把鼻子伸進小鴨子的箱子裡，碰到小鴨冰冷的小嘴。他用鼻子摩擦已經變冷的熱水袋，感覺到這隻小小的小鴨子正抵著他的臉頰，他用腳掌輕輕地將紙箱翻過來，讓奇奇爬出紙箱，躺在他的下巴底下睡覺。

paw
[pɔ]
名 腳掌

tip
[tɪp]
動 翻倒

Ted noticed that he had an **extra serve** of **cereal**
for breakfast, and he did not mind at all
if Clackymucky paddled in it.
What he *did* mind for the first few days
was the newspaper that suddenly
appeared on the floor.

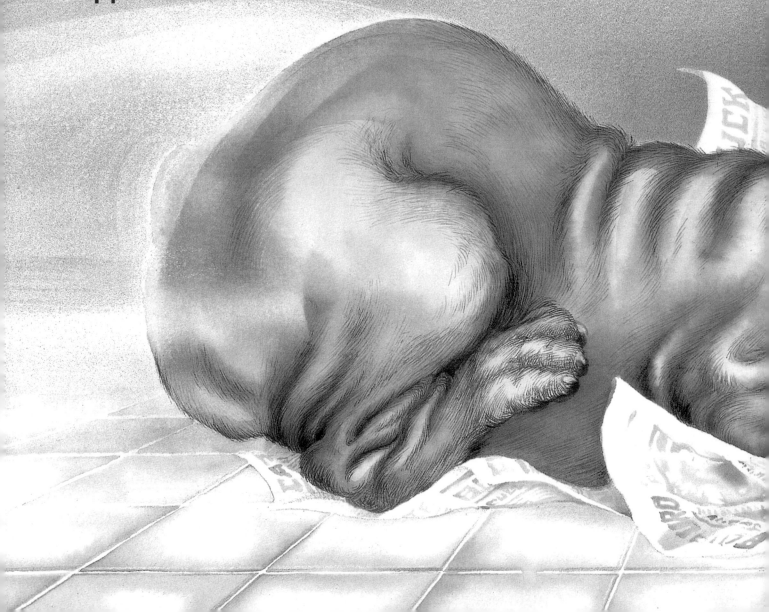

As soon as it became **wrinkled** and nicely **smelly**, it was **gathered up** and **replaced** with new sheets that **slid** from under his paws.

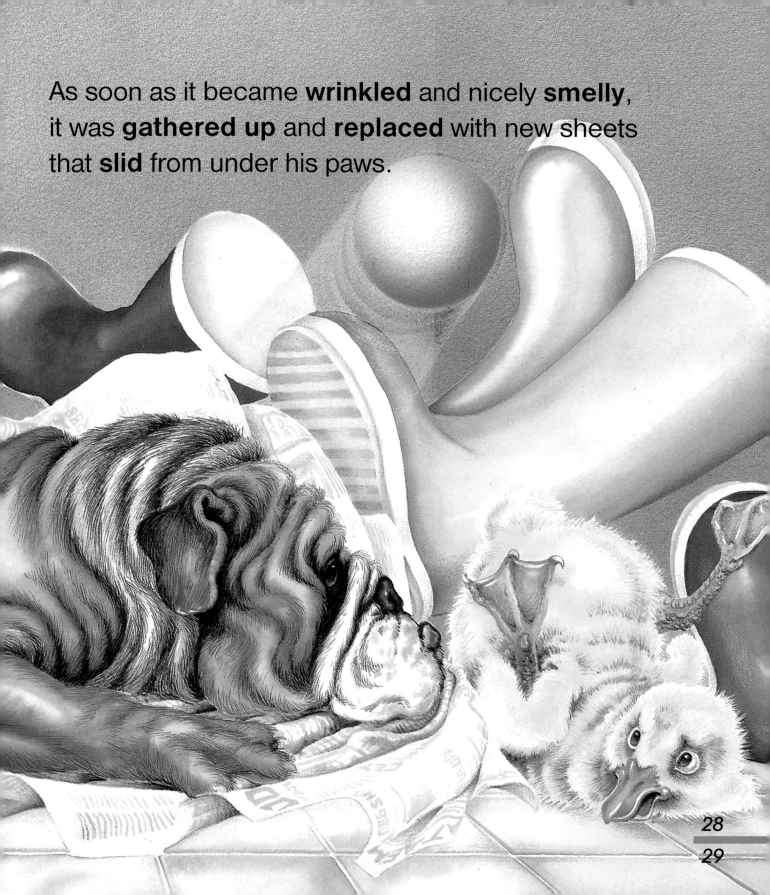

extra
[`ɛkstrə]
形 額外的

serve
[sɝv]
名 招待

cereal
[`sɪrɪəl]
名 穀類

appear
[ə`pɪr]
動 出現

泰德注意到他的早餐多了一份麥片，而且他一點都不在意奇奇爬到他的麥片粥裡玩耍，剛開始那幾天，他真正在意的是地板上忽然出現的報紙。

只要報紙變得縐縐的，聞起來臭臭的，就會被收起來丟掉，再從他的腳掌底下鋪進新的報紙。

Ted and Clackymucky played for hours each day.
Ted taught her to play with a ball.
He taught her to play with a shoe.
And when it was time for his afternoon snooze,
she **slipperydipped** down his head!

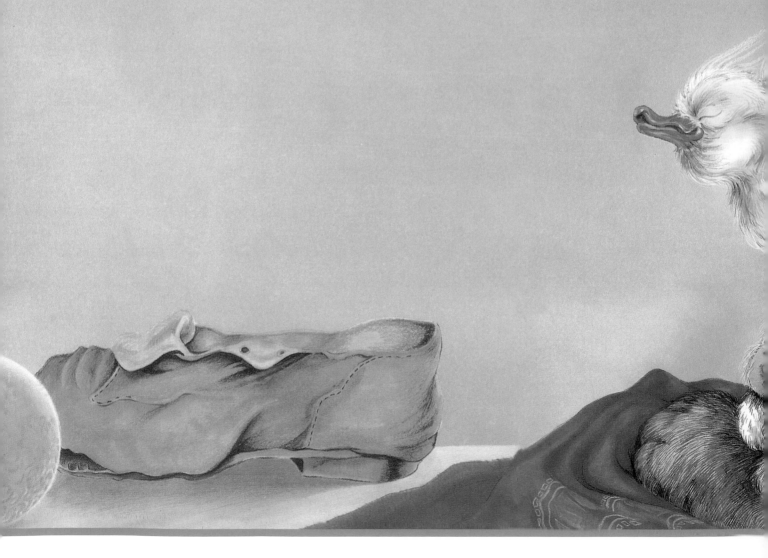

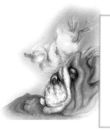

slippery
[`slɪprɪ]
形 滑溜溜的

dip
[dɪp]
動 下降

每天，泰德都要陪奇奇玩上好幾個小時。泰德教奇奇玩球，也教奇奇玩鞋子。在泰德睡午覺的時候，奇奇便會從他的頭上「咻！」地滑下來。

Clackymucky grew very fast
and white **feathers sprouted** through her **down**.
She ate chick-**crumbs** and boiled egg yolk,
green peas and flies.
One evening she **spotted** her very first 'worm'.
Clackymucky had never seen a worm before.
She ran to it and **grabbed** it.
She shook it and dropped it.
She **tossed** it and caught it.

Then, to Ted's great surprise, she *ate* it!

feather
[ˋfɛðɚ]
名 羽毛

sprout
[spraʊt]
動 成長

down
[daʊn]
名 絨毛

crumb
[krʌm]
名 碎屑

spot
[spɑt]
勔 發現

奇奇長得好快喲！身上冒出一根一根的白色羽毛。她吃飼料、熟蛋黃、青豌豆，還有小蒼蠅。有天傍晚，她見到了生平第一隻「蟲」。奇奇以前從沒見過蟲子長什麼樣子。她跑過去啄起那隻蟲子，搖一搖，甩到地上，再咬起來，往上一拋，然後用嘴巴接住。

然後，令泰德大吃一驚的是，她把蟲子吃掉了！

grab
[græb]
勔 攫取

toss
[tɔs]
勔 向上拋

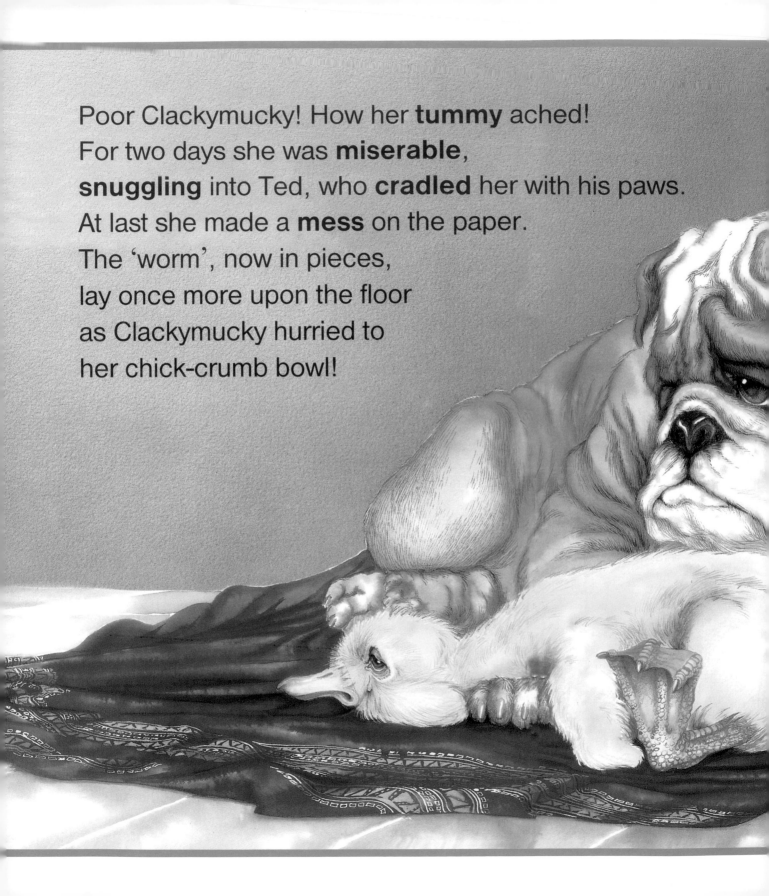

Poor Clackymucky! How her **tummy** ached!
For two days she was **miserable**,
snuggling into Ted, who **cradled** her with his paws.
At last she made a **mess** on the paper.
The 'worm', now in pieces,
lay once more upon the floor
as Clackymucky hurried to
her chick-crumb bowl!

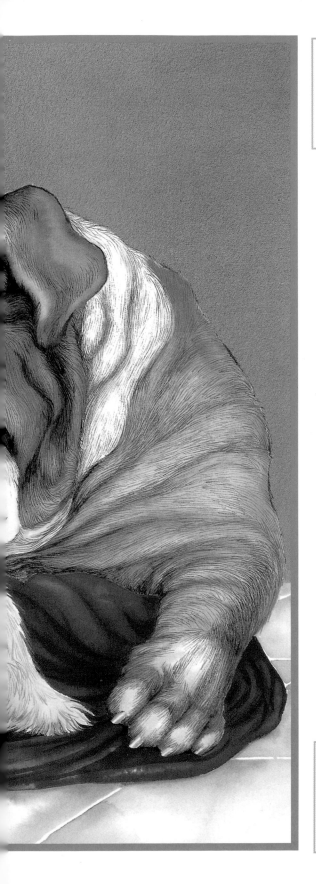

tummy
[`tʌmɪ]
名 肚子

miserable
[`mɪzrəb!]
形 痛苦的

snuggle
[`snʌg!]
動 貼近

可憐的奇奇，她的肚子好痛啊！
她整整病了兩天，縮在泰德的懷
裡，泰德輕輕哄拍著她。最後她
終於稀里嘩啦地吐了一地。奇奇
迫不及待地衝向她那裝飼料的小
碗，而那隻「蟲」這會兒可是零
零落落地散落在地板上。

cradle
[`kred!]
動 哄抱

mess
[mɛs]
名 排泄物

One morning Clackymucky followed Ted outside.
When Ted walked down the path she followed him.
When he walked through the **pot plants**
she followed him and there she found her first **snail**.
Then she heard a new sound.
"Quack-quack-quack!" came Daphne's voice
as she called to her **brood** on the pond.
Clackymucky was **puzzled**.

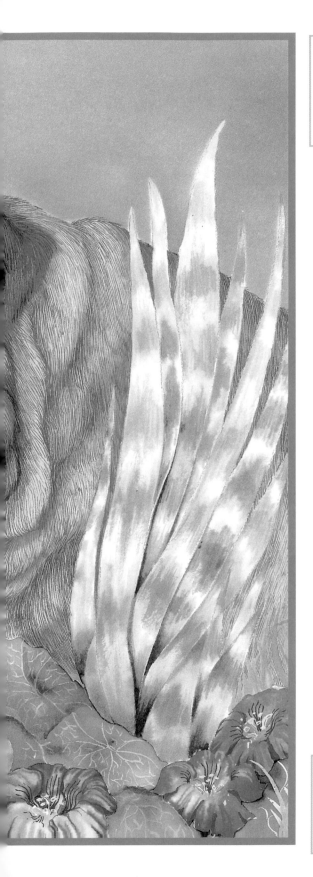

pot
[pɑt]
名 盆

plant
[plænt]
名 植物

有天早上，奇奇跟著泰德出門。她跟在泰德後面，沿著小徑往下走，經過一叢盆栽的時候，奇奇第一次見到了蝸牛。接著她聽到一個新奇的聲音 ，「呱—呱—呱！」那是妮妮在呼叫池裡的鴨寶寶。奇奇有些困惑。

snail
[snel]
名 蝸牛

brood [brud]
名 同窩孵出的雛禽

puzzled
[ˋpʌz!d]
形 困惑的

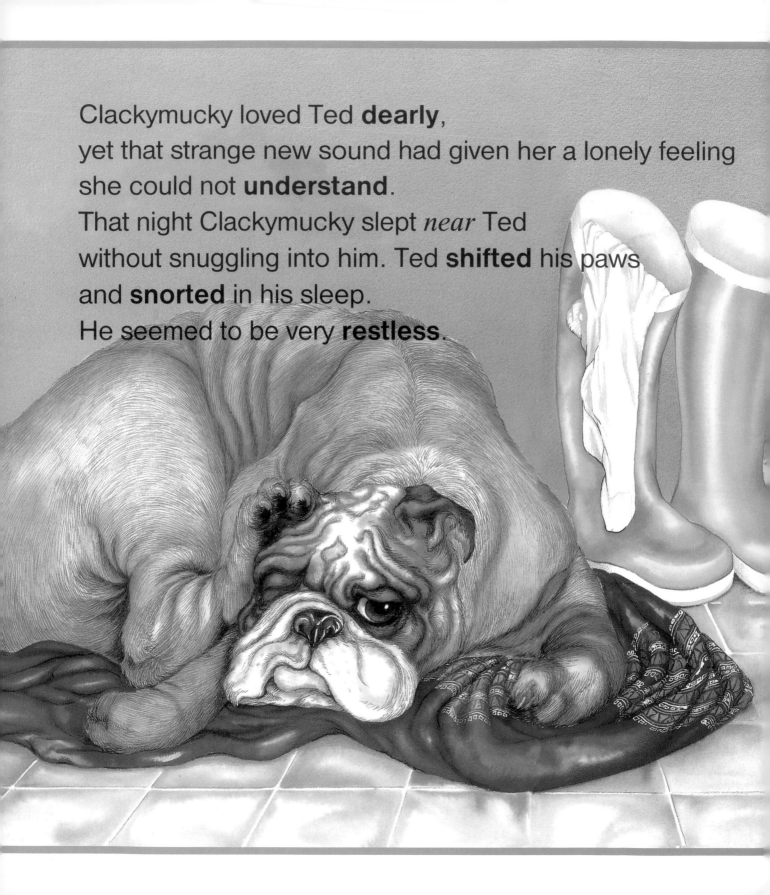

Clackymucky loved Ted **dearly**,
yet that strange new sound had given her a lonely feeling
she could not **understand**.
That night Clackymucky slept *near* Ted
without snuggling into him. Ted **shifted** his paws
and **snorted** in his sleep.
He seemed to be very **restless**.

dearly
[`dɪrlɪ]
副 深情地

understand
[ˌʌndɚ`stænd]
動 理解

奇奇好喜歡泰德，可是那陌生而新奇的聲音，讓她感覺到一種自己也不能理解的孤獨感。那天晚上，奇奇沒有鑽進泰德的懷裡睡覺，她睡在泰德身邊。而泰德一下子翻來覆去，一下子吐著大氣，似乎睡得並不安穩。

shift
[ʃɪft]
動 移動

snort
[snɔrt]
動 噴鼻息

restless
[`rɛstlɪs]
形 無法安眠的

42

43

Next morning, Ted sat in the doorway
until Clackymucky had finished her third bowl of food.
When she joined him he led her outside.
Not to the pot plants. Not to his tree.

隔天早上，泰德坐在門口等奇奇吃完第三碗食物。等奇奇來到他跟前，便領著她向屋外走去。今天他們不到盆栽叢那兒，也不到泰德的樹下。

Ted led her down to the pond.
Clackymucky stopped at the edge of the pond
where her **webbed** feet **slipped** in the mud.
The ducklings swam in a circle and stared.
"Quack!" said Daphne.

Then Clackymucky knew what to do.
Into the water she jumped.
"Quack," she said softly.
"Quack-quack-quack!"

Proudly she looked across at Ted.
The old bulldog **winked** at her.

webbed
[wɛbd]
形 有蹼的

slip
[slɪp]
動 滑倒

wink
[wɪŋk]
動 眨眼示意

泰德帶著奇奇到池塘那兒，奇奇在池塘邊停了下來，她那雙有蹼的小腳害她在泥巴上滑了一跤，小鴨子們游成一圈盯著她看，「呱！」妮妮叫了一聲，奇奇便知道該怎麼做了，她跳進水裡，輕輕地叫著：「呱！呱！呱！」她驕傲地望向岸邊的泰德，這隻老鬥牛犬正對著她擠眼睛呢！

Then he turned to walk to his **favorite** tree
where the bees buzzed in nasturtium flowers,
and he could lie on the grass and snooze
in the far, far corner of the garden.

favorite
[`fevərɪt]
形 最喜愛的

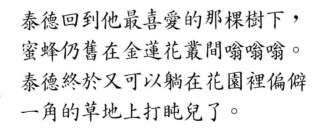

泰德回到他最喜愛的那棵樹下，
蜜蜂仍舊在金蓮花叢間嗡嗡嗡。
泰德終於又可以躺在花園裡偏僻
一角的草地上打盹兒了。

我愛阿瑟系列

英漢對照系列
看故事學英文

I Love Arthur

■ 阿瑟做家事　　　　■ 阿瑟找新家　　　　■ 永遠的阿瑟

阿瑟是一隻最不起眼的小黃狗，為了討主人歡心，
他什麼都願意做，但是，天啊！
為什麼他就是一天到晚惹麻煩呢！？
一連三集，酷狗阿瑟搏命演出，
要你笑得滿地找牙！

他練習游泳、吐氣泡，還有在水中呼吸，他很努力地練習著，直到他確信，自己可以當條金魚。

Amanda Graham・Donna Gynell 著　本局編輯部編譯

英漢對照系列
看故事學英文

農場裡的小故事

別害怕！羊咩咩！

羊咩咩最討厭夜晚了，
到處黑漆漆的，
還有很多恐怖的黑影子，
而且其中一個黑影子
老是跟在他後面……
羊咩咩怎樣才能不再害怕黑影子呢？

快快睡！豬小弟！

上床時間到了，
豬小弟還不肯睡，
他還想到處玩耍，
可是大家都不理他，
他只好自己玩……

有一個農場，
裡面住著怕黑的羊咩咩、
不肯睡覺的豬小弟、
愛搗蛋的斑斑貓

和愛咯咯叫的小母雞，
農場主人真是煩惱啊！
他到底要怎麼解決
這些寶貝蛋的問題呢？

別吵了！小母雞！

小母雞最愛咯咯叫，
吵得大家受不了，
誰可以想個好法子，
讓她不再吵鬧？

別貪心！斑斑貓！

斑斑貓最壞了，搶走了小狗狗的玩具球，
扯掉豬小弟的蝴蝶結，
還吃光了農夫的便當……
她會受到什麼樣的教訓呢？

Moira Butterfield 著　Rachael O'Neill 繪圖　本局編輯部 編譯

小普羅藝術叢書

我喜歡系列

創意小畫家系列

小畫家的天空系列

創意小畫家系列
榮獲聯合報《讀書人》版年度最佳童書！

當一個天才小畫家
發揮想像力
讓色彩和線條在紙上跳起舞來！！

一共１５本，教你怎麼用面紙拼貼、
畫各種風景、動物，
還有冰淇淋哦！！

國家圖書館出版品預行編目資料

小鴨奇奇和鬥牛犬 = Clackymucky and the bulldog
　/ Josephine Croser 著；Carol McLean–Carr 繪；
　三民書局編輯部譯－－初版．－－臺北市：
　三民，民88
　　面；　公分
　ISBN 957–14–3010–2 （平裝）

　1.英國語言－讀本

805.18　　　　　　　　　　　　　88004003

網際網路位址　http : // www. sanmin. com. tw

ⓒ 小鴨奇奇和鬥牛犬

著作人　Josephine Croser
繪圖者　Carol McLean–Carr
譯　者　三民書局編輯部
發行人　劉振強
著作財　三民書局股份有限公司
產權人　臺北市復興北路三八六號
發行所　三民書局股份有限公司
　　　　地址／臺北市復興北路三八六號
　　　　電話／二五〇〇六六〇〇
　　　　郵撥／〇〇〇九九九八——五號
印刷所　三民書局股份有限公司
門市部　復北店／臺北市復興北路三八六號
　　　　重南店／臺北市重慶南路一段六十一號
初　版　中華民國八十八年十一月
編　號　S85460
定　價　新臺幣壹佰玖拾元整
行政院新聞局登記證局版臺業字第〇二〇〇號

有著作權　不准侵害

ISBN　957–14–3010–2 （平裝）